O9-BSU-041

WITHDRAWN

BRIGHT EYES,
BROWN SKIN

by Cheryl Willis Hudson & Bernette G. Ford
Illustrated by George Ford

PZ
7
H858
Br
1990

124794

Text copyright © 1990, by Cheryl Willis Hudson and Bernette G. Ford. Adapted from the original poem, *Bright Eyes, Brown Skin* copyright © 1979 by Cheryl Willis Hudson. All rights reserved. Illustrations copyright © 1990 by George Ford. No part of this book may be reproduced or utilized in any form or by any means, electronic or mechanical, including photo-copying, recording or by information storage and retrieval system without permission in writing from the publisher. Inquiries should be addressed to JUST US BOOKS, INC., 301 Main Street, Orange, NJ 07050.

Printed in Italy. First Edition 10 9 8 7 6 5 4 3 2 1
Library of Congress Catalog Number 90-81648
ISBN: 0-940975-10-6 (lib. ed.)   0-940975-23-8 (paper)

JUST US BOOKS
Orange, New Jersey
1990

**Bright eyes,
Brown skin...**

A heart-shaped face,

A dimpled chin.

Bright eyes,

Cheeks that glow...

Chubby fingers,

Ticklish toes.

A playful grin,

A perfect nose…

Very special
Hair and clothes.

Bright eyes,

Ears to listen...

Lips to kiss you,

Teeth that glisten.

Bright eyes...

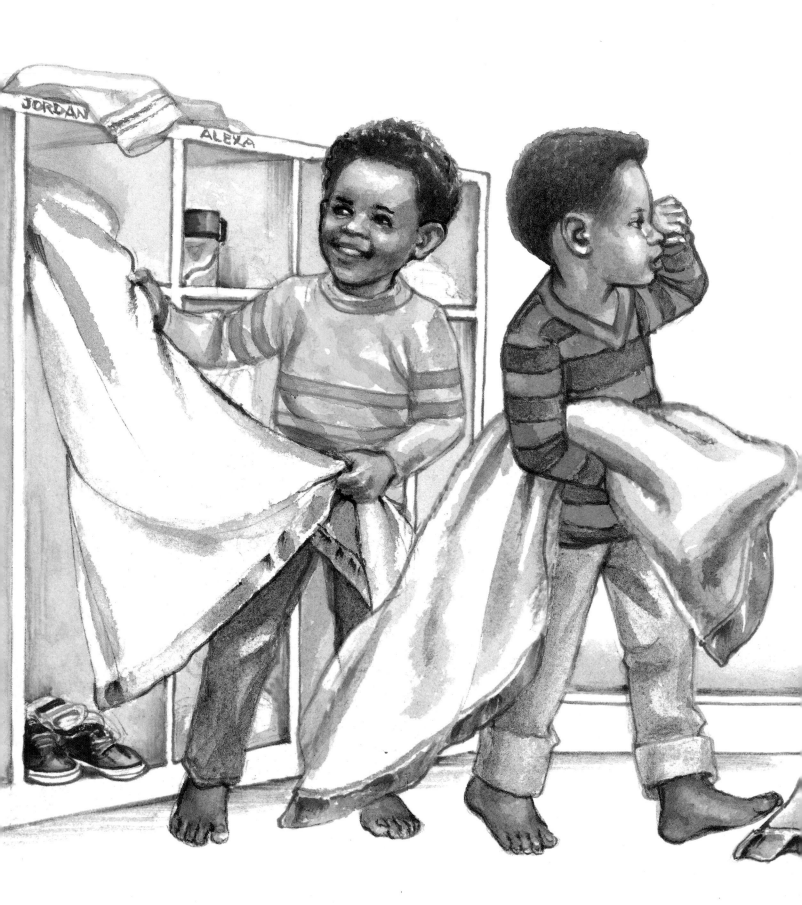

Brown skin...

Warm as toast,

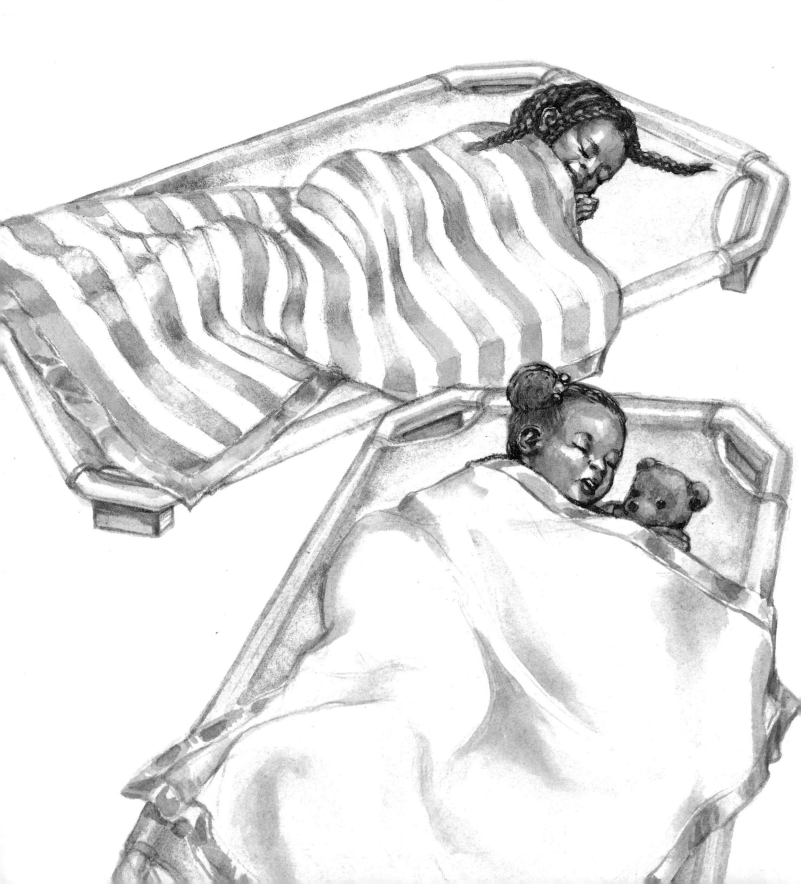

And all tucked in.

Olivia

Jordan

Ethan

Alexa

CHERYL WILLIS HUDSON is an author and graphic designer of children's books. *Afro-Bets® A B C Book* and *Afro-Bets® 1 2 3 Book* were her first published titles and her poems, stories and illustrations for children have appeared in *Ebony Jr!* and *Wee Wisdom Magazine.* She has designed many books for major publishing companies, as well.

Ms. Hudson, a native of Portsmouth, Virginia, graduated from Oberlin College in Ohio. She now makes her home in New Jersey with her husband, Wade, and two children, Katura and Stephan.

BERNETTE G. FORD is a publishing executive at a major New York children's book company. Under a pseudonym she has written several books for young readers during the course of her career as an editor. Ms. Ford grew up in Uniondale, New York, and graduated from Connecticut College for Women.

This is the first book on which she and her husband George have collaborated, but it is not the first time their daughter, Olivia, has appeared in George's pictures. Ms. Ford, George and Olivia live in Brooklyn, New York.

GEORGE FORD is a distinguished artist who has illustrated more than two dozen books for young readers. He grew up in the Brownsville and Bedford-Stuyvesant sections of Brooklyn and spent some of his early years on the West Indian island of Barbados. Among the books Mr. Ford has illustrated are *Afro-Bets® First Book About Africa, Muhammad Ali, Far Eastern Beginnings, Paul Robeson, Ego Tripping* and *Ray Charles,* for which he won the American Library Association's Coretta Scott King Award.

3 1200 00124 794 8

PZ
7
H858
Br
1990

124794
Hudson, Cheryl Willis
Bright eyes, brown skin

DATE DUE

SEP 14 1993		
JAN 1 1 1994		
JAN 2 5 1996		
MAR 0 5 1996		
2 A V		
DEC 0 6 1996		
DEC 0 4 1998		
FEB 0 7 2002		
FEB 0 4 2002		
FEB 2 7 2003		
MAR 0 3 REC'D		
FEB 7 2007		
FEB 2 8 2007		

DEMCO 38-297